To
Evelyn,
Merry Christmas!
Love,

. . . .

'Twas the night before Christmas,
when all through the house,
Not a creature was stirring,
not even a mouse;
Evelyn's stocking was hung
by the chimney with care,
In hope that St. Nicholas
soon would be there.

Evelyn was nestled all snug in her bed,
While visions of candy canes danced in her head.
And Mom in her kerchief, and Dad in his cap,
Had just settled down for a long winter's nap.

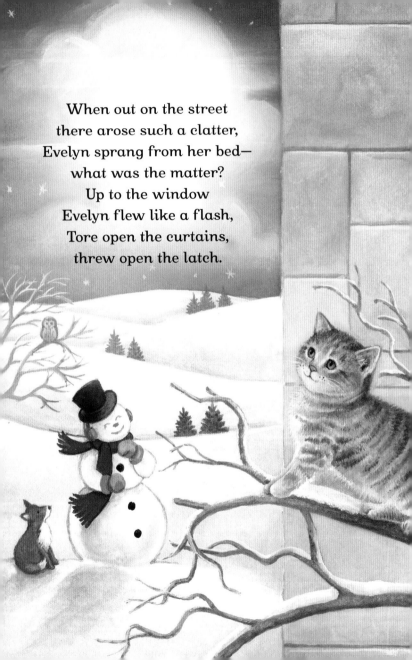

When out on the street
there arose such a clatter,
Evelyn sprang from her bed—
what was the matter?
Up to the window
Evelyn flew like a flash,
Tore open the curtains,
threw open the latch.

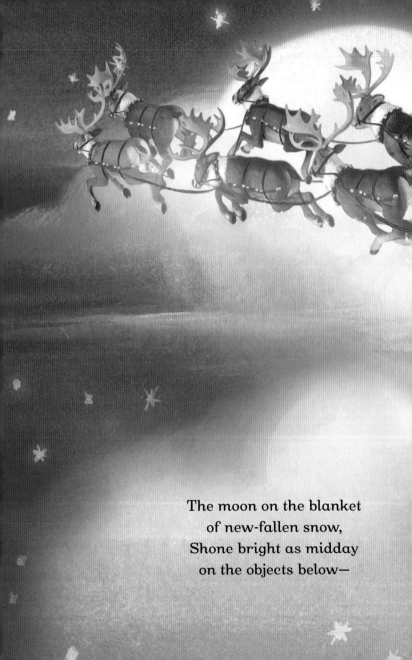

The moon on the blanket
of new-fallen snow,
Shone bright as midday
on the objects below—

When, what to Evelyn's
wondering eyes should appear,
But a miniature sleigh
and eight tiny reindeer.

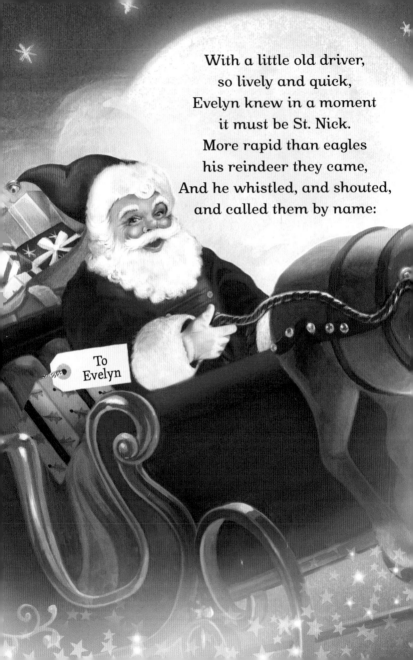

With a little old driver,
so lively and quick,
Evelyn knew in a moment
it must be St. Nick.
More rapid than eagles
his reindeer they came,
And he whistled, and shouted,
and called them by name:

To
Evelyn

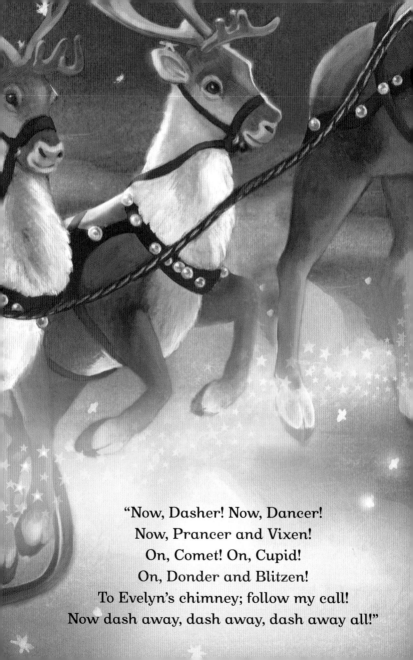

"Now, Dasher! Now, Dancer!
Now, Prancer and Vixen!
On, Comet! On, Cupid!
On, Donder and Blitzen!
To Evelyn's chimney; follow my call!
Now dash away, dash away, dash away all!"

Then, in a twinkling,
Evelyn heard on the roof
The prancing and pawing
of each little hoof.

Evelyn pulled in her head
and was turning around,
Down the chimney
St. Nicholas came with a bound.

He was dressed all in fur,
from his head to his foot,
And his clothes were all tarnished
with ashes and soot.
A bundle of toys he had
flung on his back,
And he looked like a peddler
holding his pack.

To
Evelyn

His eyes—how they twinkled!
His dimples—how merry!
His cheeks were like roses,
his nose like a cherry.
His droll little mouth
was drawn up like a bow,
And the beard on his chin was
as white as the snow.

Dear Santa,
I hope you enjoy
the sweet treats.
Love,
Evelyn
P.S. The carrots
are for your
furry friends.

A big sack of toys
he held tight in his fist,
He glanced to see Evelyn
on top of his list.
He had a broad face
and a little round belly
That shook when he laughed,
like a bowl full of jelly.

Evelyn

NICE LIST
Evelyn
Jane
Stacey
Elana
Lola

He was chubby and plump,
a right jolly old elf;
Evelyn laughed when she saw him,
in spite of herself.

A wink of his eye
and a twist of his head,
Let Evelyn know
she had nothing to dread.

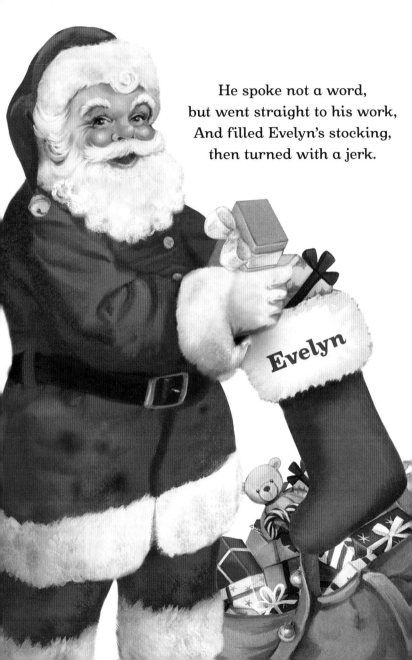

He spoke not a word,
but went straight to his work,
And filled Evelyn's stocking,
then turned with a jerk.

Evelyn

And tapping his finger at the side of his nose,
And giving a nod, up the chimney he rose.

He sprang to his sleigh, to his team gave a whistle,
And away they all flew like the down of a thistle.
But St. Nicholas exclaimed, as he drove out of sight—

"Merry Christmas, Evelyn, and to all a good night!"

Evelyn, draw all your favorite Christmas presents from Santa.

Adapted from the poem by Clement C. Moore
Illustrated by Lisa Alderson
Designed by Jane Gollner

Copyright © Hometown World Ltd. 2019

Put Me In The Story is a
registered trademark of Sourcebooks, Inc.
All rights reserved.

Published by Put Me In The Story,
a publication of Sourcebooks, Inc.
P.O. Box 4410, Naperville, Illinois 60567-4410
(630) 536-1104
www.putmeinthestory.com

Date of Production: July 2019
Run Number: 5015191
Printed and bound in Italy (LG)
10 9 8 7 6 5 4 3 2 1

MIX
Paper from
responsible sources
FSC® C023419
www.fsc.org

put me
in the story
Bestselling books starring your child!
www.putmeinthestory.com